KANSAS CITY, MO. PUBLIC LIBRARY
0 0001 5207216 1

P9-DIE-067

MAIN

iMANi
and the FLYiNG AFRiCANS

written by JANiCE LiDDELL
illustrated by LiNDA NiCKENS

Africa World Press, Inc.
P.O. Box 1892
Trenton, New Jersey 08607

Africa World Press Inc.
P.O. Box 1892
Trenton NJ 08607

Book Production coordinated at Africa World Press, Inc. by Carles J. Juzang

First Printing, 1994

Library of Congress Cataloging - in - Publication Data

Liddell, Janice.
Imani and the Flying Africans / Janice Liddell : illustrated by Linda Nickens.
p. cm
Summary: On the trip from Detroit to Savannah to see his grandparents and great grandmother for the first time, an African -American boy hears the story about an amazing event witnessed by his great-great-grandmother when she was a slave.
ISBN 0-86543-365-8 (hardcover) : $14.95. – ISBN 0-86543-366-6 (pbk.) : $6.95
[1. Afro-Americans--Fiction. 2. Slavery--Fiction.] I. Nickens, Linda, ill. II. Title.
PZ7.L613Im 1994
[Fic] – dc20
93-45806
CIP
AC

Printed in Hong Kong by Annboli and Bornmore Limited

Dedicated to my parents, Lee and Euneda Liddell:
my sons, Trae and Jelani; my grandchildren, Christy and Jahi

JL

Dedicated to my parents, Plato and Lillian Nickens;
my sister, Nancy; my nephew, Lamont and niece, Brandi

LN

"Mama, how much farther we got to go? I'm tired." The little boy , whose name was Imani and whose name meant faith , opened the super hero comic book that was in his lap. "I read all the comic books a thousand times already. This is boring."

Imani's mama smiled. Hadn't her son offered this same complaint ever since they had crossed the Michigan state line into Ohio? Now they were in Georgia, only one hundred and seventy miles from home.

"We'll be there in no time, Imani. Probably just before dark."

"How much longer that gon' be?" asked the boy.

She didn't say almost three hours, instead...she said to him, "Why don't you ask me some more riddles?"

Mother and son were driving since early morning and Detroit was a long way behind them. The south Imani had never visited, grandparents he had never met and a great grandmama who was very, very old were just a few hours away.

"How come you didn't never take me down south to visit Bigmama and Bigdaddy and Granny before Daddy left?"

"Is that your riddle?" Imani's mama asked.

"No, Mama, but I want to know."

"Well, sometimes, baby, people move away from the folks they love the most. Sometimes it's because they're angry or ashamed or just because they want to try to make it on their own. So sometimes they move away from home and all the things they know best just to prove a point."

She looked into his wide brown eyes, then turned her eyes back to the road.

"We think it's going to be just for a little while and the next thing we know years have passed by. In my case a lot of years."

She tousled his coily hair. "You know, they didn't even know they had a good looking grandson until I sent the telegram last month."

"Were they glad they have a grandson?" asked Imani.

"I told you a hundred times how excited they were when they called. You talked to them. I should ask you 'Are they glad to know they have a grandson?' "

Imani laughed and asked again, "But when are we going to get there?"

His mama ignored the question. "Well, if you won't ask me a riddle, I'll tell you a story my mama used to tell me when I was little. You know, I had forgotten all these old-timey stories until just now. This one was my favorite. It's the story about the Flying Africans."

"Flying Africans?" the boy looked curiously at his mother. "Can't no Africans fly, Mama!"

Mama smiled. "Just listen to the story, Imani."

"Back in the days of slavery, the slave boats would come to Savannah to drop off slaves. Savannah is located on the coast. When we get there I'll show you the ocean and some of the places where the slave ships came in. And the slave markets, too. The slavers that came to Savannah came straight from Africa. Mama told me this story and Granny's mama was there and saw it happen.

"They say that long ago in slavery time some new slaves came to the plantation that Granny's mama was a slave girl on."

Imani interrupted the story. "Granny's mama was a slave for real, Mama? I never knew we had slaves in our family."

"Boy, most of the Black people in America were slaves during slavery. That means almost all Black people have slaves as ancestors. But let me finish the story, Imani. It's a good one." She kept her eyes focused on the road and her hands on the steering wheel as she spoke.

"Anyway, on this one day the owner of the plantation brought home five new slaves. The slaves had come straight from Africa. They couldn't speak a word of English, so nobody could talk to them at all and they could only talk among themselves. But everyone could see that

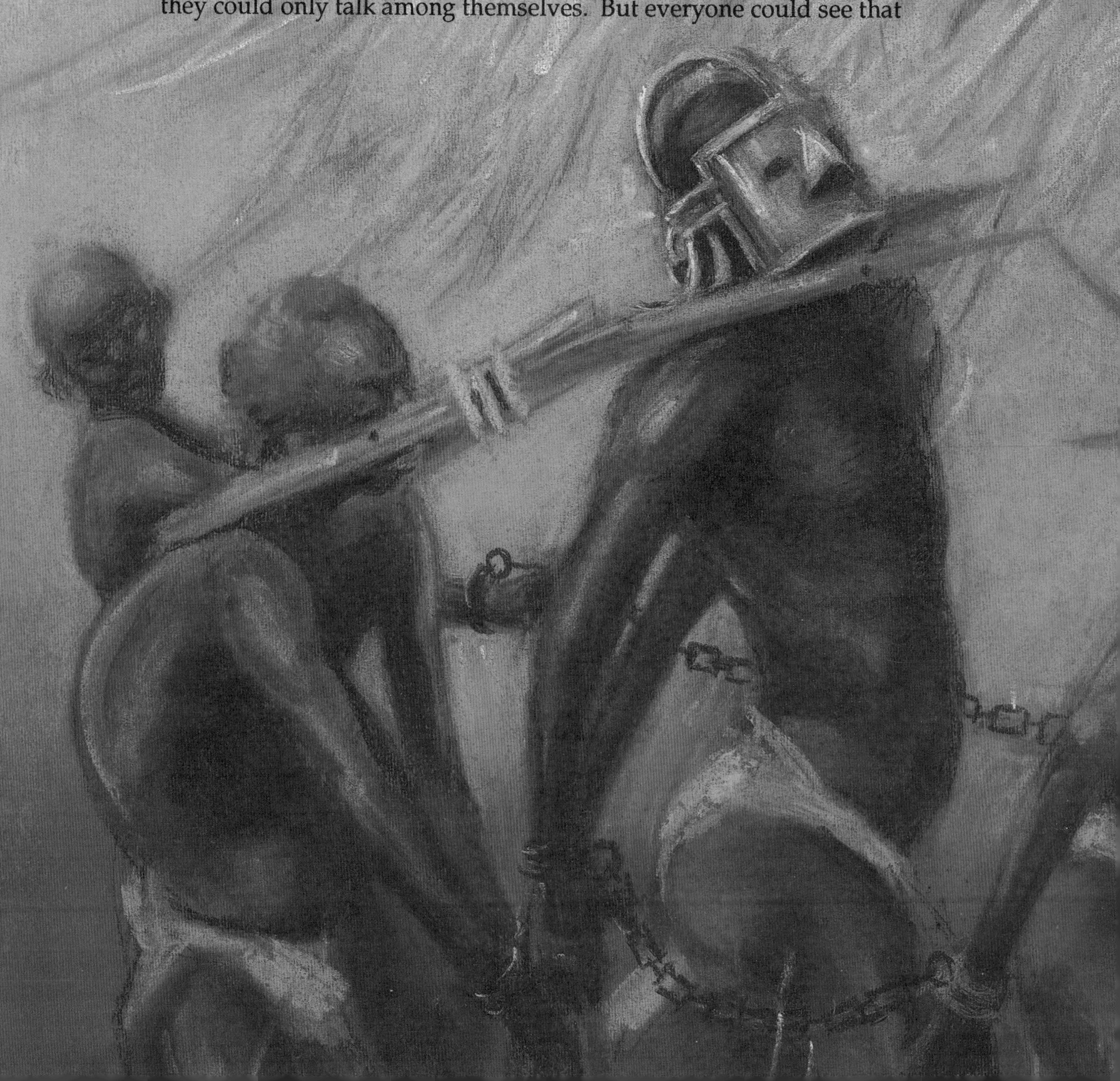

they didn't want to be where they were. They kept yanking and pulling on each other's chains trying to pull 'em off.

"And all the while they spoke in that language that nobody else could understand. The plantation owner kept them in a shed all by themselves. Everybody said he was trying to train those Africans to be good slaves. Almost everyday he would whip them and everybody on the plantation stopped what they were doing when those Africans yelled 'cause their yells would send a chill down everybody's back.

"The day finally came when the plantation owner and his overseer put the Africans into the cotton fields to work. The overseer stood by them with a gun in his belt and a whip in his hand. They hadn't been out in the field two minutes before they began to sing some song in their own language and then they started walking around in a circle. The overseer took the whip and hit one of them on the back but they never stopped walking in a circle and they never stopped singing. All the slaves in the field stopped working and began to watch the Africans. Even the overseer had lowered his whip and was watching. It was as if the song had hypnotized everybody.

"Then suddenly one of those Africans just leaped up off the ground and began to glide in the air. He spread his arms out and started to fly like a big black bird. Right after that, another one took off and then another and another until finally all five of them were high in the sky arching like a band of eagles. It looked like they

were searching for something. Granny's mama said they were looking for the way back to Africa because when the leader found what he was looking for, he took off in that direction and the rest of them followed him. They flew back to Africa. Imani, they flew back home because they were not going to be slaves. And that's the end of the story."

Imani had not taken his eyes off his mama's mouth for the last few miles. "I believe it, Mama. I believe those Africans didn't want to be no slaves. They had been packed in the slave boats and they had stood in the slave market and they saw that bein' slaves was the worse thing in the whole world. I believe they hated it so bad, Mama, that they flew—just flew right on back home. If they had tried to make me a slave, I'd a flew back home to Africa, too. We saw a movie at school about slavery and it was real bad. Yea, Mama, if I had been a slave, I'd a flew right on back to Africa." He was quiet for a few minutes. "Do you believe they flew, Mama?" he asked.

His mama smiled. "I believe they didn't want to be slaves, that's for sure." Then she noticed that the hand on the gas gauge was near E. "Well, boy, I guess we better fill up for the last time before we get back home." She began to hum a tune that was familiar and soothing to Imani. The song was one his mama had sung to him ever since he could remember. He wanted to ask mama if the song was the one the Africans sang. He wanted to ask if Bigmama had taught her the song. But the song was so sweet and his eyes so heavy. As she pulled into the gas station, she saw that her son was falling asleep. She touched his leg gently, "I'll be back, Imani; I'm going to call your Bigmama and Bigdaddy and tell them we'll be home in a couple of hours." Imani didn't answer. He had been awake since early that morning. Sleep came so easily.

While Imani's mama was on the phone and the gas station attendant pumped the gas into their car, Imani slept so soundly he barely heard the sound when the gasoline nozzle banged against the car or when the attendant sang a song about "moons" and "rivers". And when the dark car pulled into the gas station and stopped right beside their car, Imani faintly heard the car door slam. A tall skinny man got out and said something to the attendant. To Imani the voices were slow almost like a record playing on a slow speed.

Imani could hardly focus his eyes and when he did , everything seemed like a movie he was watching. He seemed to be there and not there at the same time. The skinny man and the attendant walked to the door of the gas station. They even seemed to walk in slow motion.

Before Imani could figure out what was happening, a short, fat man in a red shirt jumped out of the dark car and into their car and was driving away. Imani looked through the window for his mama. She was still on the telephone with her back to him. He screamed out the window for her and saw her turn around as the car sped away from the gas station.

The red shirt's voice was gruff. "Shut up kid, if you don't want to get hurt." Imani was afraid. The man must be a bank robber or maybe a kidnapper, he thought. Imani didn't know what to do. He looked over his shoulder and saw the gas station fading away in the distance. After a short while that seemed very long to Imani, the man said in his gruff voice, "If you cooperate, you won't get hurt." What could he mean? thought the terrified Imani.

It seemed as though they had driven quite a few miles when Red Shirt turned into a dirt road that seemed to lead into the thickest woods Imani had ever seen. Imani remained quiet but he kept sneaking glances out the window hoping to see a police car speeding up behind them like in the movies or the comic books. But he knew that once they entered these thick woods, there would be no such rescue. No one would know where they went.

MA

The car moved slowly over bumps and pot holes. The man cursed under his breath and swerved to avoid a big hole. Imani had not dared to look up into Red Shirt's face. He kept his eyes on the car door. He no longer sneaked glances out the window. It was no use, he thought. No one could find him now. Then the car stopped suddenly with a loud thud. Imani looked into the man's face for the first time. He had a scraggly beard, a tooth missing and he wore an old baseball cap. The man cursed loudly and looked at Imani as though it were his fault the tire had gone into the big hole.

"You might have to help push," the man said in his gruff voice as he opened the car door. Red Shirt walked to the front of the car and looked at the tire. He bent down below the car frame where Imani could no longer see even the baseball cap.

Now's my chance, thought Imani and he opened the car door, jumped out and ran faster than he had run the May Day relay at school.

Before the baseball cap could rise above the car frame, Imani was almost to the edge of the woods, his legs moving faster than they had ever moved. As he reached the woods, he turned back to see the man in the red shirt running after him. He was yelling something, but Imani didn't try to catch the words.

Imani was a fast runner. The man was not. Imani ran through rustling leaves, breaking sticks and branches, leaving marks and sounds that anybody could follow. Still, Red Shirt was a long way behind. Suddenly, Imani came to a clearing. There seemed to be two or three paths and he had to choose one fast. He looked over his shoulder and saw Red Shirt catching up. Imani quickly chose the path in front of him.

He was tired but his pace only slowed a little. Imani felt as though he was running for his life. He just had to reach safety no matter what. A few feet in front Imani saw a surprising sight, someone to help. It was a woman. A dark woman who was very, very old. Imani did not stop to wonder why an old woman would be sitting way out here in the woods all alone. He looked at the woman and only thought of help. He ran to her crying almost breathlessly: "Help me, please, Ma'am. There's a man chasing me. He's gonna kill me if he catches me. Please help me."

Imani looked over his shoulder and saw Red Shirt just passing the clearing. Imani did not have much time and the old woman had not moved at all. She had not even looked at Imani. Imani jumped up and down and shouted louder, "Please help me, lady! Mama, Mama...!" he screamed even louder. But, of course, his mother was nowhere around.

The woman looked at him for the first time. "A boy with the name Imani ought to know about faith. If you want to get back home, boy, just jump and fly."

Suddenly Imani remembered the tale about the Flying Africans. Yea, he could do it. He knew he could. He ran with the longest steps he could take, then jumped into the sky. Red Shirt was by the stump where the old woman sat. But the woman was no longer on the stump. Imani circled the stump and looked for the old woman. Since he was in the sky, he could see for miles, but there was no old woman. Only Red Shirt stood down below watching Imani, as though he could not believe at all what he saw. Imani spread his arms like wings of a big bird and headed into the direction of Savannah. He wasn't sure how he knew he was headed towards Savannah, but he knew. He knew he was headed towards home. He knew his mama would be there by now, would be there with Bigmama and Bigdaddy. They were all probably so worried about him.

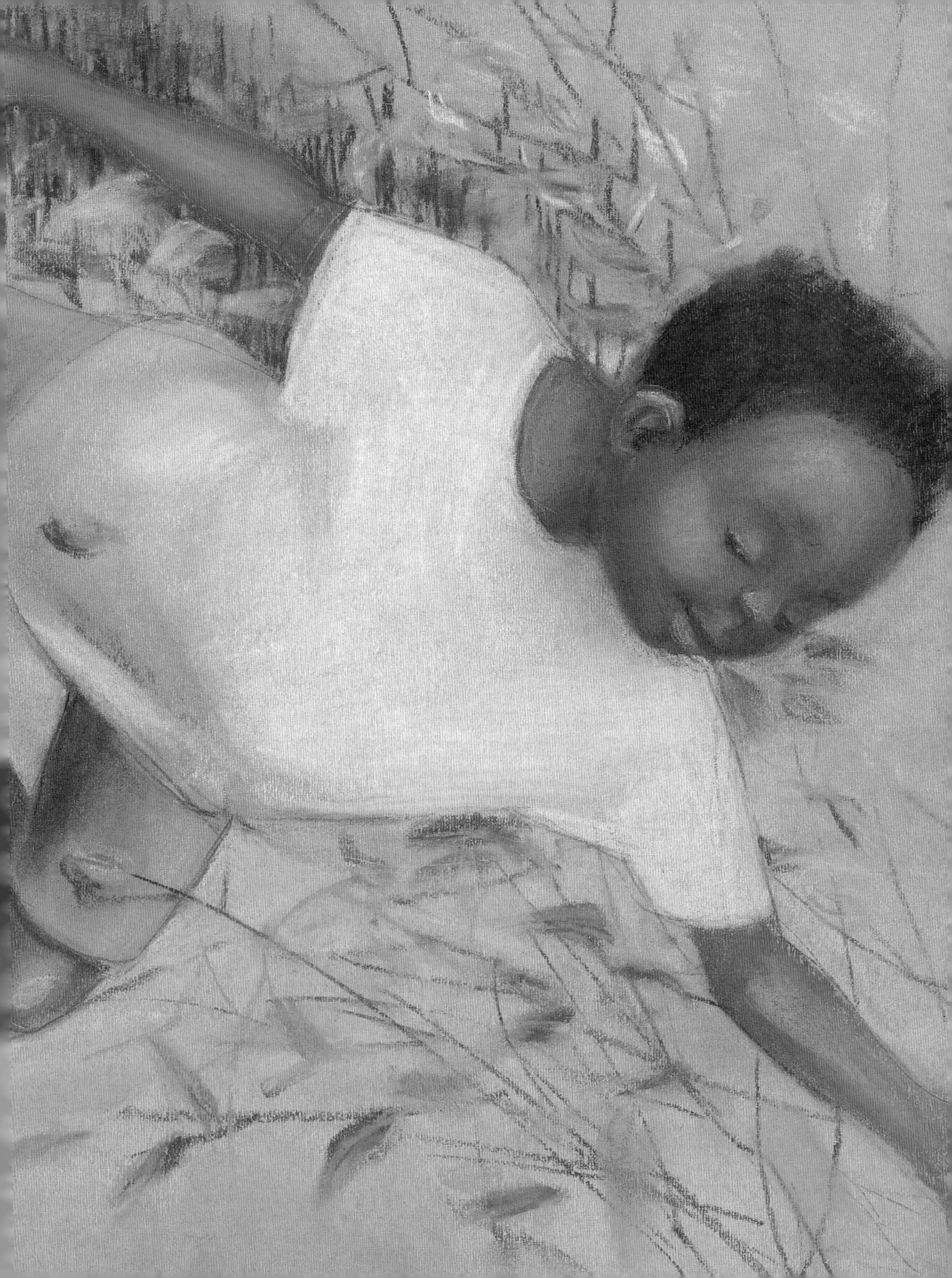

"Wake up, Imani. Wake up." It was his mother's soft voice. "We're here. Wake up and meet your Bigmama and Bigdaddy." Imani lifted his head from the man's shoulder. "Who was this? " he wondered. Had Red Shirt caught him after all? He pushed away from the big shoulders, then he saw that this man's shirt was blue, not red at all. Who was *this* strange man? Then he recognized his mother and saw her standing beside the man with her arm around a strange lady who wore a bright green apron. He looked around for Red Shirt and saw nothing red except some flowers growing beside a big tall tree in front of a strange house. He rubbed his eyes. Could it really have been a dream? His legs felt so tired and Red Shirt had seemed so real.

"Wake up, honey." His mother said again. "Give Bigdaddy a big hug and Bigmama, too." Tears were in everybody's eyes and they were all hugging and kissing. Then he remembered this must be his grandparents' house and these must be the grandparents he had never known. He forgot all about Red Shirt and the bad dream for the time being. He was finally with his Bigmama and Bigdaddy and that was much more important than a bad dream.

Then the lady spoke. "You got to come in to see Granny. She been waiting for y'all to come all day. Wouldn't close her eyes till she saw this boy here. Come on in. We can get the suitcases later."

They walked up the neat walkway that had brightly colored flowers on both sides and up some steps into a screened-in porch. Bigdaddy still carried Imani as he talked to Imani's mama. When Bigdaddy opened the screen door, Imani saw an old woman sitting in a wheelchair. Imani's mouth dropped open. He knew this old woman. She was the same woman from the dream, the same woman on the tree stump. She was the same old woman who had told him to fly. He couldn't believe his eyes. Imani wanted to jump down and hug her.

"Mama," it was Bigmama talking to the old woman, "this is your great grandson, Imani." Granny looked up at Bigmama like she was crazy. "Well, I guess I know my own great grandson," she said slowly. She reached a thin hand out and held Imani's small hand tightly—and Imani knew he had really arrived home.